Books are to be returned on or before
the last date below.

13 NOV 2012

3rd copy 26/2/19

LIBREX-

Children's
Books

a division of Hodder Headline Limited

For my mate Michael and Saoirse Ruby, of course.

"A horse! A horse! My kingdom for a horse!"
– Richard III.
"Sounds like a fair swap, Dickie!"
– Detective Gloria Van Hay-Ward.

Text copyright © 2002 J. J. Murhall
Illustrations copyright © 2002 Gary Swift

First published in Great Britain in 2002
by Hodder Children's Books

The rights of J. J. Murhall and Gary Swift to be identified as the
author and illustrator of this work respectively have been asserted
by them in accordance with the Copyright, Designs and
Patents Act 1988.

10 9 8 7 6 5 4 3 2 1

A Catalogue record for this book is available from the British Library

ISBN 0 340 84346 2

Printed and bound in Great Britain by
Bookmarque Ltd, Croydon, Surrey

Hodder Children's Books
A division of Hodder Headline Limited
338 Euston Road, London NW1 3BH

ROLL CALL: 91478 HORSE FORCE

GUS BARNS
Height: 16 hands   Colour: Grey
Age: 7
Comments: A gentle giant, slow and dim.
An orphan who was brought up on a horse
sanctuary. Happens to be accident-prone
(hence long delay in passing police
training course).

CALVIN DE CANTER
Height: 14 hands   Colour: Piebald
Age: 5
Comments: A real drama queen. Longs to
work undercover, which is why he sweeps
into the squad room every morning
wearing new accessories as a disguise.
All teeth and angst.

MADDOX MANE
Height: 14 hands   Colour: Chestnut
Age: 10
Comments: Tough-talking and wild, Maddox
is the brightest and bravest of the
bunch. A former circus performer, he's a
bit of a loner and can be quite a dark
horse at times.

LOUIS REINS

Height: Debatable - strictly a pony.
Joined under false pretences?
Colour: Jet black with white ankle
socks.   Age: 6
Characteristics: Aside from a complex
about his height which makes him *v.*
tetchy, Reins is incredibly greedy.

KENDALL SNAFFLEBIT

Height: 15 hands   Colour: Bay
Age: 8
Characteristics: Always moaning about
something or other, Snafflebit is a
terrible pessimist, also superstitious
and paranoid. Never goes to work without
a vast collection of lucky charms, which
never bring any luck.

GLORIA VAN HAY-WARD

Height: 14-and-a-half hands
Colour: Palomino (with dyed blonde
highlights)
Age: Refuses to divulge.
Characteristics: Vain. Other officers
wary because she can be forthright and
is also well-built. Most of her leads
come via her hairdresser - a gossipy
kangaroo called Andrea.

Chapter One
Squad Room Squalor

Chief Inspector Harry Krupps threw open the door to his office and scowled across the noisy squad room floor. There was no doubt about it and it was no use pretending: he loathed his new job. This extremely grizzly bear was bad-tempered and impatient at the best of times, but as Officer-in-Charge of the Creature Crimes division of Prospect Hill police station, he found his new job very trying indeed.

The canine department upstairs was fine. Those Dog Squad dogs were excellent detectives, each and every one.

The Goat Herd officers on the ground floor weren't as competent, but at least they tried. As for this lot in front of him – the Horse Force – what a complete and utter shambles they were.

He surveyed the scene in disapproval. A group of horses lounged around the room, playing cards, reading comics, or doing absolutely nothing (with their hoofs up on their desks). Litter bins were overflowing. Desktops were scattered with apple cores, fizzy drink cans and sweet wrappers, and the entire floor was covered in a light dusting of hay and sugar.

Inspector Krupps sighed bitterly. This wasn't a squad room. It was a cross between a nursery and a farm and here he was, with over thirty years of loyal service to the force, babysitting a bunch of lazy, overgrown donkeys that couldn't catch their breath, let alone a thief.

Chief Inspector Krupps strode into the middle of the room. Enough was enough. It was time for some drastic action. Criminal creatures were running riot on the city streets whilst these so-called police horses sat around on their fat behinds all day, drinking coffee and cola and eating doughnuts.

"ATTENTION!" hollered Inspector Krupps above the chatter.

However, his cry fell on deaf ears. If there was one thing that the Horse Force was good at it was ignoring orders.

The Chief Inspector stomped over to the radio blaring on top of a filing cabinet and abruptly switched it off. Then, pulling a whistle from the top pocket of his uniform, he blew shrilly on it. A flurry of playing cards shot into the air as a detective called Kendall Snafflebit dropped the pack in alarm.

"ATTENTION, 91478 – HORSE FORCE!" Inspector Krupps yelled once again.

The chatter died down and the horses stared back at him with a mixture of shock and irritation.

"All right. Keep your fur on. There's no need to shout," muttered Detective Louis Reins, putting down his fifth hay and pickle sandwich of the morning and rubbing his ringing ears. He didn't like old cranky Krupps one bit. Ever since he'd arrived at the station, the Inspector hadn't stopped goading him about his height, insisting that he couldn't possibly be a horse – he simply wasn't tall enough. "You're nothing but a short fat pony, Detective Reins. And you'll never, *ever* be anything else."

These harsh words almost broke Louis' heart. It was his life-long regret not to have grown up to be a lofty and elegant thoroughbred racehorse.

"Right, you lazy lot. Gather round. I'm calling an urgent meeting," the Chief continued gruffly. He wheeled a large flip chart to the middle of the room and picking up a long thin baton, he briskly pointed to the words written on the front page in thick felt pen:

CITY'S MOST WANTED

The horses glanced warily at each other as Chief Inspector Krupps flipped over the pages of photographs. They showed head-and-shoulders shots of a haughty giraffe, a scowling pig, a shifty polar bear, laughing cats and dogs, even a coy kitten peeping over the rim of a flower-filled wicker basket. He flipped over another page to reveal a grainy passport booth snapshot of a group of sneering squirrels – four grey and one red, with his tongue poking out.

"This cheeky bunch are the city's latest recruits into the world of crime," announced the Chief Inspector gravely. "They go by the name of the Broken Claw Gang, led by the red one – Ginger Whelks. A right little hooligan, if ever I saw one."

The horses nodded in agreement. Detective Kendall Snafflebit's shoulders slumped. He could feel a case coming on. He hated having to go outdoors and solve crimes. He would much rather have stayed in the squad room where it was safe and warm.

"Now, they may look young – but don't be fooled by those cute furry faces," the Chief continued. "These little bushy-tailed bandits have been digging up flower beds in back gardens and tipping over window boxes throughout the city over the past week. But now they're bored with terrorizing innocent gardeners. They've set their sights on bigger things." He tapped the picture with his baton. "Prospect Park is now under siege by this despicable gang of teenage tearaways. The public can't use the park without fear of being picked on. We've had reports of ankle-biting, pushchair-pinching, peeing in the paddling pool and ice cream sabotage. The park warden is too scared to leave his hut, ever since the little horrors chased him into the sand pit and buried him up to his neck."

Louis Reins put up a hoof. "What sort of ice cream sabotage?" he asked eagerly. Louis loved talking about food.

"They've broken into the ice cream van on two occasions and mixed salt and pepper in with the ice cream and substituted tomato sauce for strawberry and gravy for chocolate," the Chief Inspector replied in distaste.

Detective Reins licked his lips. He thought it sounded delicious, but then Louis Reins would have probably eaten a lawnmower if it was cut up and served to him on a plate with a side order of chips.

"There are also reports of some serious playground equipment-tampering going on as well," said Chief Inspector Krupps gravely. "Superglue on the slide, sawing through swings – that sort of hazardous thing."

Detective Gus Barn, the Horse Force's biggest recruit, rubbed his backside and winced.

"Imagine getting glued to a slide," he remarked. "You'd have to uproot the whole thing and carry it around attached to your bum for ever. How embarrassing."

The other horses nodded. Chief Inspector Krupps looked annoyed.

"Right, if we could continue, please. You lot have a new case to crack and you've no time to waste. The Dog Squad is far too busy to take this crime on at the moment. They've got four awards ceremonies to attend and a knighthood to pick up this week."

The horses looked sullen. Detective Spencer "Just call me Flash Dog" Studs and his cronies were always solving crimes and being rewarded for it. It was so annoying.

"Anyway. The last known hideout for Ginger and his mob was the third oak tree on the left, near the bandstand. However, when the Goat Herd arrived at dawn this morning to arrest them, the gang had already done a bunk, leaving nothing behind but a burnt-out tree trunk, a broken TV set and a few stolen acorns."

"Perhaps they've gone on holiday?" remarked Kendall hopefully. "That means we might as well forget the whole thing."

Everyone ignored his casual remark. Detective Calvin de Canter leant back in his chair. Dressed in another of his many undercover disguises – a gold sparkly halter-neck top (very unflattering on such broad shoulders), droopy aviator-style sunglasses and a small ginger wig that lay between his ears like a slumbering gerbil – he removed his glasses and chewed on them thoughtfully.

"Now, how do you know that those acorns were stolen, Chief? Clawprints, I suppose?" he asked, nodding slowly and narrowing his gaze like he'd seen those flashy dog detectives do.

The Chief Inspector shook his head and flipped over another sheet to reveal a huge blown-up photograph of an acorn the size of a rugby ball. Stamped on it was the name and address of a squirrel that lived in an adventure playground across the other side of the city.

Calvin lurched back in his chair, almost tipping over.

"Err! Who's that ugly mug?" he exclaimed. "He's a right shifty-looking character if ever I saw one."

"It's not a who, it's an acorn, you idiot!" the Inspector snapped impatiently.

Calvin looked embarrassed and hastily put his sunglasses back on.

"Oops! Sorry, my mistake," he replied sheepishly. "I thought it was some sneaky crim wearing a cheapo mask. Anyway, Chief, don't you worry," he added brightly. "We'll catch those fuzzy-tailed fiends. I could go in undercover disguised as a bush, or better still – a tree. A few branches attached to my arms and a mouthful of leaves and no one will ever suspect." He pointed towards the picture. "I could even wear that giant acorn head as well, if you like." Then he looked around at his fellow officers and stated proudly, "They don't call me Camouflage Calvin, the King of Concealment, for nothing, you know."

Chief Inspector Krupps rolled his eyes in exasperation and growled softly under his breath.

"Yes, well, that won't be necessary, de Canter. However, I *do* want you all to go to the park, make some routine tree-to-tree enquiries, see if you can find out where the little devils are hiding out now. Keep your eyes open. Surveillance: that's what's needed. A twenty-four-hour, round the clock guard on the place. The gang tend to do most damage under cover of darkness. So it looks like this will be an all-night vigil."

Kendall Snafflebit shuddered. He didn't like going out after dark. He was usually in bed by seven-thirty, tucked up with a hot water bottle and his favourite teddy bear. He didn't want to be traipsing about some park in the freezing cold.

The Chief stared critically at each horse in turn. "This is your big chance to finally shape up and actually solve a crime," he said. "If you lose many more cases then I'm afraid your hoofs won't touch the ground. You'll be giving piggy back rides down at the local riding stables quicker than you can say, 'Spencer Studs is a top dog', understood?"

The horses nodded seriously. Then – standing briskly to attention – they saluted.

"OK. Gather your badge and shoes," ordered Inspector Krupps, "and remember, 91478 – Horse Force: the streets out there are mean, so it's up to you to keep them clean."

The horses hastily set about gathering up their belongings. Louis Reins pulled out his desk drawer and, after tipping it upside-down, shook it enthusiastically. Half-eaten portions of this and chewed-up bits of that spilled out over the already messy desk.

"Ah! Here it is!" he declared triumphantly, pulling out a star-shaped silver badge made from a crumpled Chinese takeaway container. Giving it a lick he pinned it proudly to his forelock. Embossed on the front were the initials "H.F." and around the edge was the motto: "In The Horse We Trust".

Next he picked up a belt that was

hanging over the back of
his chair and slung it
around his waist.
Attached to
it were four
highly-polished
silver horseshoes.
Incredibly
magnetic, these hoofcuffs were used
to catch and detain suspects.

SPARKLE

Finally, the squad was ready and
Chief Inspector Krupps made his way
down the line, inspecting the shine on
each hoof and badge critically as he
went. He was relieved to see that Calvin
had now changed into his proper
uniform. However, he tutted crossly
when he realized that one member
of the Force was missing.

"Where's Van Hay-Ward?" he
snapped. "An urgent appointment
with her hairdresser, I suppose?"

The other horses nodded. Gloria Van Hay-Ward – the force's only female member – was a law unto herself. She'd turn up for duty when she was good and ready, and not before. Appearance was everything to Gloria, and that meant always looking her best. Her hoofs were perfectly manicured, her mane well-groomed, and she wore a bow on her forelock – a different colour each day, depending on her mood.

Chief Inspector Krupps reached the last horse in the line and frowned. Big Gus Barn was standing to attention with a broom under one arm and a dustpan and brush under the other.

"What's with the cleaning equipment, Barn? You're about to go out on an important crime-busting assignment, not tidy up the staff canteen."

"Well, sir – you told us to keep the streets clean," replied Gus, his chest

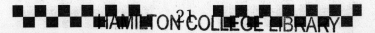

swelling with pride. "So I thought I'd make a start. I'd have taken the vacuum cleaner as well, only there's nowhere to plug it in outside, especially in a park," he added glumly.

Inspector Krupps looked furious and snatched the implements from the big horse's grasp. In his opinion Detective Barn was a half-wit: nothing more than an overgrown  carthorse. He should be pulling a plough, not trying to solve crimes.

He looked at the rest of the team despairingly. "Just get out there and at least *try* and catch a culprit this time, will you?" he hollered and, turning on his heel, padded slowly back to his office and slammed the door.

Inspector Krupps could feel a horse-sized headache coming on and not even an aspirin the size of a stable was going to shift it.

Chapter Two
Pranks in the Park

"**O**h don't be so ridiculous, Louis. How could someone possibly *move* a dirty, great big park?" declared Maddox Mane, shaking his head in amazement.

Louis Reins leant against the bonnet of the squad car and folded his arms defiantly.

"Well, I reckon its been shifted, 'cos I'm positive it used to be further over there." He pointed towards some buildings in the far distance. "And that's why it's taken us nearly four hours to find it."

Kendall Snafflebit rolled his eyes in despair. "It's taken us this long because you have no sense of direction, Louis. You've led us on a mystery tour – where the only mystery is, how on earth did you ever manage to pass your driving test?" he remarked crossly, stamping his hoofs to keep warm.

Louis scowled.

"Well, never mind, 'cos we're here now," Gus said brightly. "And we've got crims to catch, remember."

Kendall looked moody. "The only thing I'll be catching is a cold. It's freezing out here," he mumbled, tightening his woolly scarf.

"Gus is right," Maddox added. "It's no use squabbling. We've still got a few hours of daylight left to do some questioning. Come on." And he trotted briskly off towards the huge iron gates that led into the park.

The others followed, with Kendall reluctantly bringing up the rear. He was just dreaming of duvets and dozing and steaming hot mugs of drinking chocolate when suddenly something leapt out of the bushes behind him.

"What kept you?" a familiar voice called out. The horses stopped in their tracks and whirled around.

"Gloria! You frightened the life out of me," exclaimed Kendall, glaring at the glamorous police horse.

Gloria Van Hay-Ward stood in the middle of the path, swinging her saddle-shaped shoulder bag. Her newly-styled blonde mane and pale blue ribbon shimmered in the twilight.

"I've been hiding in those bushes for hours," she declared, pointing towards some shrubbery. "As soon as I got your call, I left the salon – didn't even bother with a manicure – and came straight here. I've been waiting for those little culprits to put in an appearance."

"I'm sorry, Gloria, but Louis was driving and he took a few wrong turnings," replied Maddox.

"Yeah, about three hundred," Kendall added sullenly.

Gloria shook her head and tossed her silken locks. "Well, never mind.

At least you're here now. Whilst I was hiding I had a very interesting conversation with a stray dog, actually. He said that he definitely saw those squirrels last night. They smashed a window of the cafeteria, grabbed some bottles and then chucked them in the boating lake."

Maddox looked thoughtful as he sifted through a nearby rubbish bin.

Calvin pressed his eye up against a hole in a tree trunk. "I can't see a thing," he mumbled. "It's blacker than my mad Aunt Mabel's stable in there." He put his sunglasses back on and plonked himself down on a park bench.

"Well, at least we know that they're still in the area," said Maddox. "What's the betting that as soon as it gets dark they'll be up to their old tricks again?"

He bent down and peered under the bench. Then, pulling a piece of chalk out of his pocket, he carefully drew a ring around an empty crisp packet and a few smaller ones around some crumbs.

"Um, I don't think you should be drawing all over the path, Maddox," Gus said worriedly. "I don't want to have to arrest you for defacing park property."

Detective Mane glared. "This crisp packet could be vital evidence. I'm just marking the spot so that we can dust it for prints later on."

Gus sighed heavily. "I *knew* I should have brought my duster along."

"Not *that* sort of dusting!" snapped Gloria. "Honestly, Gus Barn, don't you know *anything* about police procedure?"

"Not really," shrugged Gus. "I know how to do paw and claw printing. I'm quite good at that," he said. "And I can say 'STOP THIEF!' really loudly," he added brightly. "But apart from that, I'm afraid I failed all my exams. I think they only let me join the Horse Force 'cos I kept on pestering them."

The other horses looked at him fondly. It was true. Gus really was the Horse Force's dimmest recruit.

"Anyway, they could be hiding anywhere, lying in wait for us," Maddox continued, putting his chalk back in his top pocket. "We must be on our guard at all times, gang. I think we ought to split up. Louis – you and Calvin can go and have a word with the park keeper. See if he's seen the Broken Claw Gang hanging around recently. Have you got your notebooks at the ready?"

They both nodded. Calvin proudly pulled his notebook out (with "Party Animal" printed across it), along with a fluffy green biro.

Maddox nodded approvingly. "Good. Meanwhile, Gus and I will question a few of the park's residents, see if they've seen anything suspicious –

especially around the boating lake."

As the horses paired off, Gloria looked indignant. "So that means I'm stuck with Mr Misery Guts here, I suppose?"

Kendall scowled from behind his scarf. "Charming. I love you too, Gloria."

Gloria sighed. "Listen, Kendall. If we're going to hang out together you need to liven up a bit. Be sharp. Stay alert. I've also thought of something that'll keep you warm."

Kendall looked hopeful. "Oh, goody! Does that mean we're going to sit in the park keeper's cosy hut and toast our tootsies by an open fire?" he asked eagerly.

"Now don't be silly, Kenny, darling. We'll never catch a crim like that, will we?" replied Gloria, delving into her enormous shoulder bag and pulling something out.

"Why have you brought your pyjamas along?" Kendall frowned at the fluffy pink suit that Gloria was holding. "Are we having a sleepover?" he asked, perking up again. "I love sleepovers. I use to have them all the time when I was a little foal."

"This isn't nightwear, Kendall. It's a tracksuit," Gloria replied huffily. "A designer one, actually." She put it on.

Calvin tried not to laugh. The suit was very unflattering. Gloria looked all pink and wobbly in it, like a gigantic jelly on hoofs.

"We're going jogging, Kendall. It will be the ideal way to blend in. Think about it. Two keep-fit fanatics enjoying an evening run together. Who'll ever suspect that we're really hot-shot detectives on the lookout for disobedient squirrels? Come on." And with that she trotted off.

The other horses began to wander away, leaving Kendall watching Gloria's enormous tracksuited figure disappear into the distance.

He sighed. Kendall Snafflebit loathed exercise. All that jiggling about. It just wasn't healthy.

"You'd better get going, Kendall, if you're going to catch up with Gloria," Calvin called after him.

Kendall scowled. He had no intention of catching *anyone*. He sneezed heartily. Besides, he could definitely feel a cold coming on.

* * *

Detective Snafflebit waited until his colleagues had disappeared from sight and then turned and headed towards the car park. Back in the squad car there was a nice, warm travel rug. He could curl up under that. Catching crims was all well and good, but Kendall would have rather let crooks roam the city streets and parks than put his health at risk.

He tried the doors of the squad car. "Heck, it's locked," he said crossly. He looked around. The park was deserted. Not a single creature was in sight. The detective shivered and then, spotting an ice cream van parked nearby, trotted over to it and tried the handle.

To his delight, Kendall found it was open. "Now, who'd want to eat ice cream on a day like this?" he mumbled to himself as he climbed inside and settled down on the seat. "Oh well, who cares?

At least I get to have forty winks in the warm."

He stretched and yawned, then closed his eyes. Behind him, the soft buzz of the ice cream freezers began to lull him off to sleep. Kendall smacked his lips together and hummed softly to himself. Soon he nodded off and began to snore deeply.

A few moments later, muffled voices could be heard from inside the glove compartment. The door flipped down to reveal – squashed amongst the sweet wrappers and a pair of driving gloves – four furry figures.

"Cor! That was a close shave," announced Ginger Whelks, jumping down on to the passenger seat. "Bang goes our chance of mixing sand in with the raspberry ripple now."

Ginger jumped on to the back of the seat and ran along the edge of it.

Very gently, he climbed on to the top
of Detective Snafflebit's head and pulled
up his eyelids. Kendall stirred slightly
and then let out an almighty snort.
One of the squirrels, Sammy Mutton,
who was standing on Kendall's lap,
was blown backwards by the horse's
tremendous snore.

"Hey! That horse has got one
pair of powerful lungs!" he exclaimed,
picking himself up and climbing back

on to Kendall's lap. He peered up the horse's nose as the lazy detective blew an ear-splitting raspberry again.

This time, however, Sammy was ready and he nipped nimbly out of the way of its blast.

"What are we going to do now, boss?" asked Eddie Cruise Junior, who was balanced on top of the steering wheel. "How about I do a bit more graffiti? I could spray 'Broken Claw Gang Rules' all over the outside of the van, if you like."

Ginger shook his head. "Nah. We've left our tag on almost everything now. I've had a better idea." He hopped over the back of the seat and on to the freezers. "Let's turn the heater on and then defrost these. Turn the ice cream to slush. Make a real mess of things," he announced gleefully, pulling the plug out. "Turn the ignition on, Eddie."

Eddie Cruise Junior turned the keys in the ignition and the heater immediately started to work.

A few minutes later a small pool of vanilla ice cream began to seep from the bottom of the freezer and across the floor, oozing around Kendall's hoofs.

Very soon the ice cream began to melt more quickly, as the van's interior warmed up. The squirrels began to ladle the slushy liquid out, smearing it over every surface – including the top of the police horse's head.

Kendall Snafflebit, however, slept on. He was having such a lovely dream. It was a hot sunny day and he was at the seaside. He smiled and shuffled contentedly in his sleep and blew another raspberry. He was paddling in the sea and eating a great big ice cream cone – vanilla, his favourite.

Chapter Three
Dressing-up Drama

"**W**hat do you mean – *strip*?"

The park keeper – a sluggish, overweight bull – stared at the two Horse Force detectives standing before him.

"You heard me. I'm confiscating your uniform for undercover purposes," Louis Reins said brusquely.

The bull reluctantly began to unbutton his jacket. "This is all highly irregular," he grumbled. "I'm not supposed to lend my uniform to anyone. It's against park regulations."

Calvin raised his eyebrows. "Listen,

mate. I specialize in undercover surveillance work. Why, only last week I had to borrow a fire-dog's uniform to spy on Neville the Neck, the gentleman giraffe burglar. I even confiscated his hosepipe. If a cop orders you to surrender your uniform, you must obey."

The park keeper glanced warily at a garden hose curled up in the corner. "Well, you're not getting your hoofs on my equipment," he said gruffly. "That's park property. No one's authorized to use it except me."

"Quit stalling, will you?" ordered Louis. "We're not interested in that, just your gear."

The bull glowered as he stripped down to a pair of stripy underpants and a string vest and stood sullenly clutching his uniform. Calvin reached out and took it from him.

"Er, excuse me," remarked Louis

indignantly. "But I think you'll find that's mine." He yanked it from Calvin's grasp.

Detective de Canter bristled. "Um, actually, I think you'll find that *I'm* the undercover expert around here." And he snatched it back.

"It's mine," said Louis, making a grab for the uniform again.

"*Mine,*" replied Calvin, tugging at a trouser leg.

The bull watched anxiously as his uniform went from one bickering detective to the other. Then he stepped in between the feuding horses and held up his hoofs.

"Listen – before my pants get ripped to shreds, I've had an idea," he declared. "Why don't you both try the uniform on and whoever fits it best gets to wear it."

"Oh, you mean like the story of Cinderella and the glass slipper? What a good idea," declared Calvin, excitedly clapping his hoofs together. "Me first." And he quickly clambered into it.

Louis sniggered as Calvin tried desperately to hold up the waistband of the huge trousers. "Too big," he smirked. "Hand them over."

Calvin reluctantly took off the uniform and watched guardedly as Louis then tried it on for size.

"Ta-da! It's a perfect fit. Tailor-made," declared Louis Reins, twirling around.

Detective de Canter's expression darkened as he seethed with jealousy. "It's not fair," he complained, stamping his hoofs and snorting angrily. Tears welled up in his eyes and his bottom lip trembled. "*I* wanted to wear the disguise." He burst into tears.

"There, there. Don't cry, Mr Detective," said the park keeper, patting Calvin tenderly on the back.

Louis rolled his eyes in exasperation as Detective de Canter flung his arms around the bull's big neck and wept even louder.

"Perhaps you could dress up as somebody else, Calvin?" Louis suggested. "You know how good you are at thinking up disguises."

Calvin slowly raised his eyes from the park keeper's shoulder and peered at his colleague with red-rimmed eyes. Then he blew his nose on the bull's string vest before straightening himself up.

"You're right. Pretending to be a park keeper's boring, anyway. I bet I can come up with something far better. After all," he said, walking over to the door, "I *am* Calvin de Canter, the King of Concealment." And with his nose in the air he trotted outside.

"You must excuse my colleague," said Louis, following hastily. "He's actually a brave and fearless police horse, you know."

"Really?" the park keeper said sarcastically. He strolled over to the door and watched the two horses head off in opposite directions, shaking his head in disbelief. Then he turned back and shook his fist angrily at Louis. "Oi! What do you think you're doing? Leave those roses alone," he bellowed, as Louis started to nibble on a nearby bush.

"That's private property. If you're hungry eat some grass, like horses are supposed to."

Louis looked up, his cheeks now stuffed with petals. He swallowed hard and hastily put a rose behind his back.

"I'm sorry, but I was feeling a bit hungry," he said sheepishly. "Actually, I hate grass. Can't stand the taste of it. It's much too green and spiky and always gets stuck in my throat."

He shuddered. "Dreadful stuff."

Louis then held up the rose and waved it jovially at the park keeper. "Now these, on the other hoof, are truly delicious," he announced.

And then with one clean bite, Detective Reins bit off the top and carelessly tossed the stalk away.

Chapter Four
Jogging Jinks

"What's happening? Can you see anything, Ginger?"

Sammy Mutton looked eagerly up at his leader, Ginger Whelks, who was perched on top of a signpost in the middle of the park. Night had fallen on Prospect Park and the squirrels – Ginger, Sammy, Charlie Pie and his cousin, Eddie Cruise Junior – had come out to play.

Ginger squinted into the darkness. "Yeah, it looks like the short fat one – Detective Reins – has dressed up as old Bully the park keeper and at the moment he's busy eating all the rose bushes. And the horse in the shades has just trotted off towards the statues." He chewed thoughtfully on his gum and raised himself up to get a better view. "Uh-oh. Time for some action, boys. Looks like the one in the trackie is heading this way."

The squirrels sniggered as they heard Gloria approach, puffing and panting. Quickly, Ginger turned the sign around so it pointed in the opposite direction.

"Quick, *hide!*" hissed Ginger, shimmying down the post. He leapt into a nearby litter bin. The others followed just as Gloria drew level with the signpost.

"Goodness me, Gloria, you *are* out of shape!" Detective Van Hay-Ward rested a hoof against the signpost to catch her breath. "You really need to renew your gym membership, dear girl."

Gloria stepped back and looked up at the sign. It was hard to read in the dark, but she could just make out what it said.

"'To the Boating Lake,' hmm?" pondered the police horse. "Now, I definitely don't want to be heading *that* way. Not if I don't fancy a midnight swim, anyway." She trotted away.

A few moments later Louis looked up from his snack, and Maddox and Gus stopped their questioning, when they heard a resounding splash and then Gloria's bellowing voice echoing around the park. "Who put this darned lake here?"

The trees shook, birds took flight and nocturnal creatures ran for cover. Then, four furry faces peeped over the top of the litter bin.

"Nice one, Ginger," chuckled Charlie Pie. "Do you think she's angry about ending up knee-deep in sludgy cold water?"

Ginger climbed out. "Sounds like it," he sniggered, before dashing across the park in search of another detective to play about with.

"Oh, Uncle Bertie, what have they done to your nose? Your hair? Your beautiful big teeth?" implored Calvin de Canter as he surveyed the damage to the statue of Sir Bertram de Canter – his great-great-uncle, and founder of the Horse Force.

Standing on a plinth, one hoof cocked jauntily on his hip, Sir Bertie was indeed a mess. Stuck on the end of his nose was an ice cream cornet. Great clumps of grass had been plonked on top of his head and Sir Bertie's prominent front teeth – which were his most outstanding feature in more ways than one – were exaggerated by a couple of slabs of mouldy cheese that had been shoved into his mouth.

Stepping back to survey the damage again, Calvin's face brightened as an idea began to take shape. He clapped his hoofs together. "Calvin, you're a genius. Uncle Bertie would be so proud of you."

Calvin climbed up on to the plinth and stood beside the famous statue. "Now, all I've got to do is stand very still and not move a muscle," he whispered into the statue's ear. "And sooner or later those little devils will pass by again and then I'll pounce on them." He tenderly patted his uncle's head and the grassy wig slipped over one eye.

"Now don't you worry, Uncle Bertie, because your clever nephew is a master of disguise. Just watch." And Calvin copied the same pose as his Uncle.

Half an hour later, his eyelids were becoming heavy and his hoofs were beginning to ache. Calvin yawned but resisted stretching.

"Cor, being a statue is really hard work," he complained, hardly daring to move. He stifled a yawn. His fight with Louis earlier had worn him out.

A few minutes later – just like his lazy colleague snoozing back in the ice cream van – the King of Concealment was sleeping like a baby.

If Calvin de Canter had stayed awake a few minutes longer he would have seen the squirrels passing by on their way back to their latest hideout.

It was Eddie Cruise Junior who spotted him first. "Cor, look! A snoring statue," he declared, stopping and pointing up at Calvin's slumbering figure.

Ginger followed his gaze. "Don't be daft," he scoffed. "That's not a statue. That's one of those lazy police horses." He took a felt pen from his pocket. "Shall we give him a makeover, just

like his Uncle?" Ginger climbed nimbly on to the plinth and began to softly draw on Calvin's face.

When he'd finished, he jumped down and stood back to admire his handiwork. "An improvement, don't you think, boys?"

The others nodded gleefully. Calvin de Canter, the King of Concealment, was almost unrecognizable. He now had a moustache, glasses and his face was dotted with big black spots.

Chapter Five
Hosepipe
Frenzy

To say that Gloria Van Hay-Ward was angry as she emerged from the boating lake – dripping wet, like an enormous pink monster – would be putting it mildly. She was positively *fuming*.

Gloria had a temper at the best of times. Her tantrums were legendary throughout the city. First she'd quiver, then she'd stomp and then she'd start to throw things: tables, chairs, small furry animals – anything close by, really.

With her bedraggled mane and her designer tracksuit already starting to shrink, Gloria was currently at the stomping stage. However, all that was about to change as she made her way up the bank and across the park.

"Whatever's happened, Gloria?" asked Louis in surprise.

Gloria ignored him, pushing her colleague roughly to one side. She flung open the door to the park keeper's hut and observed the bull warming himself by the fire. "Where are your water sprinklers? I'm going to flush the little monsters out!" she raged.

The bull pointed towards the wall with a shaky hoof. He was, after all, dressed only in a pair of pants and a vest and was hardly in a position to argue with such a formidable-looking creature.

Gloria unravelled the hose and flicked the switches on the wall that worked the sprinkler system.

"No one messes with Gloria Abigail

Serena Van Hay-Ward and gets away with it," she seethed. "As my dear departed mummy used to say, 'Gloria,' she said, 'if you want a job done properly, send for a mare.'" She grabbed hold of the nozzle and aimed it at the bull. "Stand aside, if you know what's good for you."

The bull ducked down behind a stack of deckchairs as Gloria turned the tap on full blast and marched outside. The sprinklers were now whirling around at great speed soaking the already dewy grass.

Louis stared across at his colleague. "Gloria! What on earth are you doing? Have you gone stark staring *mad*?" he shouted. "Turn those sprinklers off and put that hosepipe back. You're soaking the place."

Detective Van Hay-Ward tossed back her mane and flared her nostrils.

Louis, recognizing that familiar wild and unhinged look in her eye, chucked aside his rose-scented supper and galloped away. The water was gushing out of the hosepipe and she aimed it towards him.

Louis Reins, his hoofs slipping on the wet grass, yelled, "Look out, everyone! Run for your lives! Gloria's lost her marbles – again."

But the warning came too late. The fuming detective was already heading across the park, dragging the hose behind her.

"Come out, come out, wherever you are!" she ordered.

Gloria stuck the hosepipe under bushes and she shoved it up a tree. She waved it around like a maniac.

A face popped out of a hole in the trunk, before disappearing back inside. Henry Rhymes (resident of Flat 12, Oak Tree Mansions) began to wake his neighbours.

"Quick! Abandon your homes. Grab what you can. Mad horse on the loose! It's a flood! A tidal wave! A monsoon!" hollered the squirrel, knocking frantically on each door in turn.

A moment later, woodland creatures including moles, rabbits and squirrels began to emerge from other trees and shrubbery, carrying whatever they could manage as Gloria continued to reek havoc with her hosepipe.

A mouse appeared from beneath
a bush carrying a battered suitcase
under its arm. As a large oak leaf
floated by on the path the animal
jumped swiftly on to it. He was soon
joined by other animals, all using
branches and empty burger cartons
as a means of escape.

Gloria watched the animals sail

up the path, tapping her hoof indignantly as she searched their faces for any sign of the Broken Claw Gang members.

"Where *are* those little villains?" she snapped. She stared down the end of her hosepipe. The torrent was now just a trickle.

"Gloria! Losing your temper is no way to catch a crim," Louis shouted, emerging from the park keeper's hut, having finally managed to turn off the sprinklers and Gloria's deadly hose.

Detective Van Hay-Ward flicked her sodden forelock from her eyes. "You're right," she sighed. "I don't know what came over me. Mummy had a ferocious temper as well. She once got so angry waiting for a set of traffic lights to change, she flattened them with a single punch."

Henry Rhymes, perched high above

their heads in an oak tree, glowered down at her. "You'll regret this. I'm calling the police."

"But we *are* the police," scoffed Gloria.

"I mean *proper* cops. Those who catch criminals. Not ones who drown innocent members of the public!" replied the squirrel, dialling 666 on his tiny mobile phone. He turned his back on the horses as he was connected to Prospect Park police station.

"Hello. I'd like to report a serious offence. One of your Horse Force officers has tried to drown the inhabitants of the park . . ."

Gloria and Louis looked at each other in alarm as the squirrel held the phone away from his ear. The distinctive voice of Chief Inspector Krupps could be heard bellowing down it. When he'd calmed down, the squirrel put the phone to his ear again.

"Yes, that's right, Chief Inspector. Our homes are completely ruined. The park will take weeks to dry out. We may even have to sue the city for compensation. Right. OK. I'll tell them. Goodbye."

The squirrel switched his phone off and regarded the detectives coldly. "Oh dear. Oh deary, deary me. Looks like the Horse Force is in *big* trouble once again. Your chief is sending reinforcements. Reckons you can't cope under pressure."

Louis and Gloria, now joined by Maddox and Gus, stared up at him.

"So who's he sending? The Goat Herd, I suppose?" asked Maddox. "They won't do much. Except eat every blade of grass and flower."

Behind him, Louis let out an enormous burp and looked shameful as he thought about all the flower stalks and petals scattered about the park.

"Oh no. The Inspector felt that the nature of this act was so severe that he's sending a team far more efficient than them," the squirrel stated proudly.

Everyone listened to the distant sound of a distinctive siren. It was a cross between a bark and a whine and marked the arrival of an infamous team of dogged detectives.

The Horse Force looked at each other, startled.

"On no! Look who it is!" wailed Gus, pointing across the park

Like a band of barking superheroes, the four silhouettes, all immaculately dressed in black cashmere overcoats, came bounding towards them.

Prospect City's finest detectives, the Dog Squad, were most definitely on the case.

Chapter Six
Sniffer
Squad

"**H**ave you just got out of the bath, Gloria?" smirked Detective Studs.

Gloria looked indignant as the Dog Squad detectives surrounded her.

"I hope you realize that we've been dragged away from a special fundraising dogs' dinner just to be here," Detective Archie Lead snarled crossly.

The squirrel looked impressed. "Who was it to raise funds for? Stray dogs, I suppose?"

"Don't be so ridiculous," Detective Lead said indignantly. "We don't believe in doing good deeds – except towards ourselves, that is. Actually, it was to raise cash to send us all on a holiday to the Caribbean."

The Horse Force looked knowingly at each other. That was typical of the selfish Dog Squad. They only ever thought of themselves.

Detective Studs began to lightly sniff the air. "Anyway, me and my colleagues don't want to be hanging around a waterlogged park all evening. There's a meal of prime steak and chips waiting for me back at the do. So I suggest we get started, guys."

The dogs began to sniff the grass around them and then, following their noses, headed towards a large pine tree further along the path.

"Look at those hounds go," remarked Henry Rhymes in admiration. "They're on the scent already."

The horses watched enviously. The Dog Squad's sense of smell was incredible. They could sniff out a suspect from half a mile away, if the wind was blowing in the right direction.

Spencer Studs stopped outside the pine tree, sniffed twice again, just to make certain it was the right address, and then knocked briskly on the trunk.

"Police. Open up!"

After a few moments a door in the trunk slowly opened and a small furry face peeped out.

Detective Studs flashed his gleaming gold bone-shaped badge at him. "Dog Squad here. You probably know

who I am. I'm in the papers every week picking up awards," he announced arrogantly. "And these are my fellow detectives: Lead, Bones and Chokechain." He leant closer towards the wizened old squirrel. "And what's *your* name?" he growled.

"Mutton. L-L-Leslie M-M-Mutton," stuttered the squirrel, clutching his threadbare dressing gown to his chest. "I'd invite you in, only the place is a mess, and besides" – he looked them up and down – "you wouldn't fit through the door."

Detective Reggie Chokechain moved towards him. "Are you trying to be funny, wise guy?" he snarled. "We know you're not alone in there. We can sense that you've got company. *Unsavoury* company."

Spencer Studs clicked his paws. "Bones, Chokechain – get round the back. Make sure the suspects don't try to escape." He turned his attention to the squirrel again as the creature sniffed dejectedly. "Harbouring a criminal is a very serious offence. You're looking at five years in maximum security, with no chance of parole. That would mean no more hibernating or nut-gathering for an old-timer like you."

The squirrel paled and nodded his head. "All right. I own up. Sammy Mutton is my grandson. He and his friends turned up this morning, looking for a place to hide out." Leslie Mutton's shoulders slumped. "They ate all my winter stash of nuts," he said despondently. "But Sammy's a good boy, really. He just got in with the wrong crowd."

Gus stared down at him kindly. "Don't worry, Mr Mutton. You won't be going to prison." He patted the old squirrel carefully on top of his head with his huge hoof.

"Yeah. But this little lot will be."

Detectives Chokechain and Lead appeared from around the back of the tree. They were holding four squirming squirrels by their tracksuit collars.

"We caught them trying to escape out of the back door," announced Reggie Chokechain gleefully.

"Naughty, naughty," said Spencer, wagging a paw at the teenage tearaways. "Now, make it easier on yourselves, boys. Have you got any stolen property hidden in the old fella's flat?"

Sammy Mutton nodded. "Just a few things."

Spencer Studs shoved his nose inside the tree trunk. "Cor, it stinks of earth and acorns in here!" he declared rudely. Then he began to toss various items over his shoulder. Soon there was a pile of household goods on the grass, including a tiny toaster, a minuscule ironing board, soggy bed linen, matchbox-sized videos and photographs of Sammy as a smiling toddler.

The Dog Squad detectives sifted through it. Then Reggie Chokechain picked up a small plastic card.

"Ah! What have we got here? A library card," he declared, waving it about. "Now this *must* be stolen. I can't ever imagine any of you lot reading a book." He sneered at the squirrels. "Who does it belong to? Come on, own up."

"It's mine, *honest*," declared Ginger Whelks. "My signature's on the back, if you don't believe me."

"Yeah, yeah, and the Horse Force are top cops too," scoffed Reggie as he flipped the card over. But sure enough stamped on the back was Ginger's name and scribbled in pencil was his signature.

"Well, well, well. The little rascal *is* telling the truth," said Reggie with surprise.

"There's an old saying," Gloria declared, "that you should never judge a book by its cover."

The dog detectives stared back at her crossly.

"I love to read, actually. When I'm not out smashing stuff up, that is," said Ginger cheerfully. "Reading's brilliant. My favourite books are the Barry Trotter ones, all about a pig wizard."

Gus looked interested. "They sound great. I'd like to read them myself."

"Well, you'd have trouble, Barn. Seeing as you couldn't even read a bus ticket, let alone a book," smirked Detective Studs.

The other dogs giggled.

"Anyway, if we've quite finished discussing boring books, I'd like to get back to our party," continued Spencer Studs impatiently.

"They'll be holding the raffle shortly. I hope to win first prize. Chokechain, Lead – take these little troublemakers back to the station and put them in a cell," he demanded. "It'll be court for this lot first thing in the morning and prison grub by lunchtime."

The squirrels began to cry. Suddenly, they looked very small and young to the Horse Force.

"But they're only kids. Couldn't we just let them off with a warning?" Maddox suggested. "I reckon they've learnt their lesson. Haven't you, lads?"

The squirrels looked on dejectedly as Sammy's grandfather handed his grandson a hanky.

"We're really sorry," whimpered Sammy. "We were bored, see. There's nothing to do in Prospect Park, except feed the ducks or climb trees. We wish there was a youth club where we could have some proper fun."

"Being young isn't about having a good time," remarked Spencer Studs severely. "Why, when I was a pup we didn't even have toys. Just an old bucket to play with. You lot have never had it so good." And he and the other dogs began to drag the youngsters away. "Come along. A spell in detention might make you see sense."

The dogs stopped in their tracks as they saw Kendall trotting towards them.

"What happened to you?" asked Gloria.

Kendall's legs and hoofs were now smothered with ice cream and he was leaving a trail across the wet grass.

"Don't ask. I almost drowned in this stuff. It was terrible," moaned Detective Snafflebit.

"Sounds great to me," Louis said, grabbing the detective's hoof and giving it a hearty lick.

Kendall snatched his hoof away and turned towards the Dog Squad. "You lot have just received an urgent call on your car radio. Apparently, Teddy Hallelujah has been spotted careering through the city in a stolen Rolls Royce," said Kendall gravely.

"We've been after that joy-riding rhinoceros for weeks," Spencer Studs said eagerly. "Come on, boys. Let's leave this baby stuff to the Horse Force. We've got bigger criminals to catch."

And with that, the dog detectives raced off across the park, coat tails flapping. The Horse Force watched them climb into their car and screech away, the distinctive Dog Squad siren barking and wailing. Then the horses surveyed the squirrels soberly.

"Please don't send them to prison," Leslie Mutton implored. "I promise to keep a closer eye on my grandson in future." He ruffled the top of Sammy Mutton's head. "You've learnt your lesson, haven't you, son?"

Sammy looked sheepishly at the ground. "Yeah, Grandad," he mumbled.

Ginger nodded. "Me, too. I've decided that I'm going to spend more time reading." Then he gave a heavy sigh. "Only I wish I hadn't been banned from the library."

Louis scowled. "What for? Defacing the books, I suppose?"

"No, nothing like that," the squirrel said hastily. "Overdue books and unpaid fines, actually."

Maddox indicated for the Horse Force to gather round. After a few minutes' discussion, the horses turned back to address the squirrels again.

"Even though Detectives Snafflebit and Van Hay-Ward are still extremely cross with you, we've decided to give you a second chance," Maddox Mane announced sternly.

Kendall and Gloria didn't look convinced. The ice cream on Kendall's legs was beginning to freeze and Gloria had realized that she'd lost her ribbon somewhere in the lake.

"However, there's one condition," continued Detective Mane.

"Anything. Just name it, sir," Ginger replied eagerly.

"You're to return your library books and pay off all your fines. You must also promise to stay indoors after dark from now on like all good squirrels ought to."

The squirrels nodded.

"Very well, then. You're free to go," said Maddox.

Leslie Mutton looked grateful as he – together with his grandson and his friends – began to pick up their belongings and take them back inside the tree trunk.

"Calvin! Where have you been? You missed all the excitement," announced Louis as his friend approached.

"Cor! I don't think much of that

disguise, Calvin. It's not one of your better ones," Gus remarked, looking him up and down.

Detective de Canter frowned. "What do you mean, disguise? It's true I've been undercover as a statue, but I didn't dress up." He yawned. "Although I'm ashamed to admit, I did fall asleep on the job."

"Well, that's when Ginger and his gang must have used your face as a scribbling pad," said Gloria, handing Calvin her compact mirror.

"Holy hoofs! Look at me!" Calvin studied his face intently.

"It's terrible," said Kendall.

"No, it isn't. It's brilliant!" Calvin grinned. "You'd never guess it was me. The next undercover case I go on, I'm definitely going to make my face up. Gloria, lend me your make-up bag."

Gloria clutched her bag to her chest. "Buy your own cosmetics, Calvin," she replied huffily. "But I wouldn't bother with lipstick if I were you. I'm afraid there isn't a shade around that would match your disgusting choice of clothes."

Chapter Seven
It's a
Dog's Life

"**O**i! Pony boy! Put your back into it!"
Spencer Studs grinned at Detective
Reins, who was kneeling down in
front of the flower-beds doing some
serious replanting.

Fresh from arresting Teddy
Hallelujah – the notorious car thief
rhino – the Dog Squad had been given
a few days' leave and were enjoying a
leisurely stroll in the park.

There was no rest for the Horse
Force, however. They'd arrived back at
the station and had been ordered by

Chief Inspector Krupps in no uncertain terms to "Get your butts back down to the park and clean it up!" He'd turned up later to survey the damage for himself and the park keeper – thankfully dressed once again in his uniform – had shown him around.

Chief Inspector Krupps solemnly shook his big shaggy head as he waded across the waterlogged grass.

"And you say one of my detectives is responsible for this?"

The bull nodded. "We've had to move at least half of the park's inhabitants to emergency accommodation. At the moment we've got badgers holed up in the local betting shop, squirrels in the supermarket and moles residing in the twenty-four-hour petrol station. They won't be able to come back until their homes have dried out – probably next spring."

The Chief looked sympathetic as he watched Gloria steamroller the grass. She was sitting on the machine, one hoof on the steering wheel, the other holding her compact mirror in which she was admiring her looks.

"Van Hay-Ward! Keep your eyes on the job!" he shouted.

Gloria threw him an angry look and put away her compact. "A girl's got to look her best, sir. Even when she's driving," she said huffily.

"But she's not the only horse who's been misbehaving," continued the park keeper. "Did you know that you've got a detective on your force who's in the habit of pinching other animals' clothes? And that fat one over there just can't keep his thieving hoofs off my rose bushes."

The Chief looked despairingly at him. "You send for the Horse Force and you send for disaster, I'm afraid. There's nothing I can do about them. These horses have been on courses, taken numerous exams and probably, except for Gus Barn, read every book on how to be a good detective that's ever been written." He shrugged. "But they're still absolutely useless. What's more, the Horse Force is actually expanding," Inspector Krupps continued.

The bull looked at him in alarm.

"We've got a new recruit back at the station. A young buck by the name of Roscoe Tack. Once the Horse Force has finished clearing up this mess, I'll order them back to the station. I want to introduce him."

The park keeper rolled his eyes in despair and, bidding a hasty goodbye, hurried back to the safety of his hut. Once inside he closed the door and locked it. He didn't intend coming out until next spring. Not if there was *another* one of those crazy horses on the loose.

"This is the life, isn't it, Kendall?" declared Gus, contentedly sweeping the path with his tail. "Doing a spot of tidying up in the great outdoors. You can't beat it."

Kendall scowled at him. Gus took a deep breath and stared across the park. "Oh, look. There goes little Ginger carrying his books back to the library by the looks of things," said Gus, pointing towards a little figure scurrying past a wall and towards the exit. "I think I'll just go and say hello." And he trotted off towards him.

Ginger Whelks was carrying a stack of library books under his arm and had a spray can in his hand. As the horse approached he quickly put the can behind his back.

"Hiya, Ginger," said Gus cheerfully.

Ginger smiled sheepishly. "Oh hi, Detective Barn. I'm just off to the library to do a bit of reading."

Gus smiled back. "You are a good boy. I knew that you'd see the error of your ways and learn to behave." Then he turned his attention to the wall behind Ginger. The squirrel gulped nervously as Gus frowned at some words that had been freshly sprayed on to it.

Ginger looked at him imploringly. "I'm sorry, Detective Barn. I know I shouldn't have done it. Only I couldn't resist having one last go."

He pulled the spray can out from behind his back and then lobbed it into a nearby litter bin.

"But I've definitely finished with all that now. The only words I'll be writing in future will be in my exercise book."

"Well, even though I don't approve of graffiti, what you've written about us is very kind," announced Gus, looking flattered.

"Is it?" said Ginger staring in amazement at the wall. He scratched his head and looked puzzled.

"Yes. I mean fancy writing that 'The Horse Force are helpful,'" continued Gus. "You really shouldn't have, you know."

A smile flickered across Ginger's lips.

"Oh that's OK, sir." He shrugged. "Um. Anyway I must be off. See you later." And he hurried away, leaving Gus staring happily at the wall.

He was joined a moment later by Kendall.

"Are you going to leave me to do all the hard work?" snapped the moody police horse.

Gus indicated towards the wall. "Look what it says, Kendall. 'The Horse Force are helpful.' Our efforts will now be recognized for ever."

Detective Snafflebit gazed at the wall and then snorted in disgust.

"Gus. It says 'The Horse Force are HOPELESS *not* HELPFUL.'" He rolled his eyes in exasperation.

Big Gus Barn looked despondent. "Pass me that mop and bucket will you," he sighed. "It looks like some *serious* scrubbing might be needed."

Kendall scowled. "A horse's work is never done," he muttered as he reluctantly set to work.

"Correction, Kendall," replied Detective Barns sharply. He was up to his elbows in soapy water. "You mean a *Horse Force* horse's work is never done."

Kendall rolled his eyes in exasperation once again and wrung out a cloth. It looked like it was going to be another long, tiring night down in Prospect Park.

Murhall

Madness!

3: RIDDLE OF A RICH RAT

Celebrity rat, Giselle D'Arc,
is missing, so the Horse Force trawls
the town's seediest bars to retrace
her last movements. When the trail
leads back to Giselle's multi-million dollar
home, the Horse Force smells
a different sort of rat. Is Giselle
playing games or is her life
in danger?

From Hodder Children's Books . . .

More

Murhall Madness!

1: DISCO INFERNO
2: ROMAN AROUND
3: GO WILD!
4: NO SURRENDER

At St. Misbehaviour's – real name St. Saviour's – the kids are in charge and keeping the teachers under control is no mean feat – especially their new Geography teacher, Mr Rugg. He's a man with a monstrous mission: to close down 7R's beloved school . . .